NOAH AND LINK

A Comfort Dog Story

by E. Merwin

illustrated by Anthony Lewis

BEARPORT
PUBLISHING

New York, New York

Credits

Cover photo, © Erik Lam/Shutterstock.

Publisher: Kenn Goin
Senior Editor: Joyce Tavolacci
Creative Director: Spencer Brinker

Library of Congress Cataloging-in-Publication Data

Names: Merwin, E., author.
Title: Noah and Link: A Comfort Dog Story/ by E. Merwin.
Description: New York, New York : Bearport Publishing, [2017] I Series: Hound
    Town Chronicles I Summary: Injured in a flood, a young boy recovers in the
    hospital and then at home with the help of a working dog trained to
    comfort victims of natural disasters.
Identifiers: LCCN 2016043976 (print) I LCCN 2016053782 (ebook) I ISBN
    9781684020133 (library) I ISBN 9781684020645 (ebook)
Subjects: I CYAC: Working dogs—Fiction. I Dogs—Fiction. I Survival—Fiction.
Classification: LCC PZ7.1.M479 Li 2017 (print) I LCC PZ7.1.M479 (ebook) I DDC
    [E]—dc23
LC record available at https://lccn.loc.gov/201604397

For more information, write to Bearport Publishing Company, Inc., 45 West 21st
Street, Suite 3B, New York, New York 10010. Printed in the United States of America.

10 9 8 7 6 5 4 3 2 1

CONTENTS

WELCOME TO **HOUND TOWN**

A Doggone Nice Place to Live!

Population:
25,000 people
20,000 dogs

CHAPTER 1

An Unexpected Visitor

Noah grabbed the remote control from the table beside his hospital bed. He pointed it toward the television on the wall and clicked. Images of Barkley, his flooded hometown, appeared on the TV. Instead of seeing cars on Main Street, he saw rescue workers in boats floating down the road.

Noah looked at the cast on his broken leg and saw the silly face his mom had drawn on it. Then he turned his head and gazed out the window as raindrops flowed down the glass. Suddenly, a bolt of lightning split the gray sky, followed by a loud rumble of thunder.

Just then, a man walked into Noah's hospital room holding a stocky little black-and-white dog. With its large perky ears and wide mouth, it looked like a bat with a big smile.

"Hi, I'm Sean. And this is Link," he said, placing the French bulldog on the nine-year-old's hospital bed. The dog, who was wearing a blue vest, immediately **nudged** Noah's arm. Then he buried his wet nose in the palm of Noah's hand.

"That's just Link's way of saying hello," said Sean.

"Are dogs allowed in the hospital?" Noah asked.

"Link is special. He's a working dog. And that's his **uniform**."

Sean pointed to Link's vest, which read, "Please Pet Me."

"Really? This little guy has a job?" asked Noah in amazement as he rubbed Link's soft, warm belly.

"Yes, Link is a comfort dog. He visits people after floods and other **natural disasters** and helps them feel better," said Sean.

Link pawed at Noah's blanket and then **burrowed** under it. He nuzzled the boy's side, which made Noah giggle.

"Are you here because of what happened to me and my mom?" asked Noah.

"Yes," said Sean softly.

Noah turned his head toward the window and looked out at the rain. He felt his chest tighten and tried to hold back tears.

"It must have been scary," said Sean.

As tears trickled from Noah's eyes, Link climbed onto his chest and licked his cheeks.

"It was," said Noah, patting Link. "My mom and I heard that a storm was coming. But our house is on a big hill. . . . She thought we'd be safe."

"Yes," agreed Sean. "Nobody expected that much water so fast."

"Then all the lights went out in the neighborhood, and water started to cover the lawn," said Noah, wiping the tears from his face.

Link stared into Noah's eyes as if he understood every word.

"I went to my room to get my backpack and Tank," continued Noah.

"Who's Tank?" asked Sean.

"He's my tortoise," replied Noah. "Well, he was my tortoise. I had him since kindergarten. But he slipped out of my hands when the water rose."

As Noah quietly wept, Link curled up on his lap. Another rumble of thunder boomed in the sky. Link's body shook slightly. "It's okay, boy," Noah said, stroking the dog's fur. "It's just thunder."

"Link is brave and strong, just like you," said Sean. "He has visited people all over the country after floods, fires, and tornadoes. We even got caught in the **tremors** of an earthquake. And through it all, he's comforted a lot of people. But, even though he's really tough, sometimes he feels afraid."

"It's okay, Link," Noah said. "I understand." Link slowly wagged his tail, and then pressed his black nose into Noah's arm.

All of a sudden, a friendly face appeared in the doorway. It was Nana, Noah's grandmother. "I see you've made some new friends," she said as she walked toward Noah's bed and gave him a hug. Link's stubby tail whipped back and forth like a windshield wiper.

"This is Link. He's a comfort dog," said Noah.

"And I'm Sean, Link's **handler**," Sean said.

"How do you both do?" she replied, smiling. "Well, I have some great news. The doctor said you can go home with me today."

"Really?" said Noah.

"Yes, you'll be staying at my house in Hound Town while your mom **volunteers** in Barkley to help other flood **victims**."

"Link and I are about to catch the bus back to Hound Town," said Sean.

"Can we give you a lift?" Nana asked.

Link gave a sharp yap. "I guess Link's already decided!" said Sean.

Nana and Sean helped Noah into a wheelchair and placed Link on his lap. Sean wheeled Noah and Link downstairs and across a big parking lot.

Outside the hospital, Noah unzipped his sweatshirt. He slipped Link inside to keep him warm, but the Frenchie popped out to sniff the moist air.

CHAPTER 2

Safe and Sound

Nana helped Noah and Link into the backseat of her red jeep as Sean put the wheelchair in the trunk.

In the car, Link wiggled out from under Noah's hoodie. He placed his front paws on the car door and looked out the window.

"What's it like working with a comfort dog?" Noah asked Sean.

"It's very **rewarding**. I get to see people smile after going through something **traumatic**. Petting Link makes people feel better and gives them hope. Noah, if you're interested, I have a great book about comfort dogs that I could give you."

"Great!" said Noah.

As Nana drove down the road, she asked Sean, "Where can we drop you and Link off?"

"We live next door to the library," Sean replied. "When we're not traveling with other handlers and their dogs around the country, Hound Town is our home base."

Nana soon pulled up to a pretty yellow house next to the library. In

the backseat, Link had fallen asleep in Noah's arms and was snoring.

"Tomorrow, Link and I will be visiting with families from your town, Noah. Would you like to join us at the library?" asked Sean. "You'll also get to meet some of the other handlers and their dogs."

"Can we, Nana?" asked Noah hopefully.

"Of course we'll be there," she replied.

As Sean opened the back door, Noah carefully passed him the sleeping bulldog. When Noah kissed Link's wrinkled forehead, the Frenchie opened his dark eyes as if to say, "So long for now."

Noah felt good to be out of the hospital and at his grandmother's house. In the living room, Nana helped Noah get comfortable on the sofa. She propped up his injured leg on three fluffy pillows. Noah soon fell asleep.

As Noah napped, he dreamed that it was dark and raining. He was back on the porch of his house with his mom, waiting to be rescued. She had her arms wrapped tightly around him. In his hands, Noah held Tank, his tortoise, who suddenly grew wings and flew away.

Noah was relieved to wake up and find he was safe in Nana's living room. Suddenly, thunder rumbled in the distance. Noah worried about Link.

Nana walked into the room carrying two steaming mugs of hot chocolate. "I hope Link isn't too afraid," said Noah to his grandmother.

"Don't worry," said Nana. She set the mugs down on the coffee table. "Link is one brave little dog. But even **courageous** dogs sometimes get afraid, just like people."

Noah breathed in the rich aroma of the hot chocolate and then took a sip.

"Oh, by the way, while you were napping, Sean stopped by with this," Nana said, reaching for a book on the shelf. "And I invited him over for breakfast tomorrow along with another handler and comfort dog."

"The book on comfort dogs!" Noah said excitedly. "I'll read it tonight. I can't wait to meet the other dogs tomorrow."

CHAPTER 3

Biscuits for Breakfast

The next morning, Noah awoke to hear the local news on the television. He heard a familiar voice and was surprised to see a reporter interviewing his mom!

"Nana, come quick," Noah called. "Mom's on TV!"

His mother and two other rescue workers were seated in a small boat with the reporter. In the background, Noah saw his house surrounded by water.

"What progress has your team been making?" the reporter asked Noah's mom.

"My team and I have been visiting every flooded house in Barkley. We want to make sure that everyone has been safely **evacuated**, including pets." The camera zoomed in on a fuzzy rabbit she held in her arms. "We found this little guy **stranded** in a house," said Noah's mom.

Just then, the doorbell rang. Nana got up and hurried down the hall. Noah was happy to hear Sean's voice at the front door.

"Hello," said Sean to Noah's grandmother. "I hope we're not too early."

"The biscuits are ready. You're just in time!" said Nana. Noah could hear the tip-tapping of Link's nails on the wood floor. When they got to the living room, Link ran straight to the sofa. Noah smiled and scooped him up. The dog started licking his chin.

"I see Link got right to work," said Sean.

"Yep," replied Noah. "When it comes to making people feel good, Link is a pro!"

A woman appeared in the doorway. She held the leash of a beautiful golden retriever who wore the same blue vest as Link.

"Noah," said Sean, "I'd like to introduce Keisha and Angel, another comfort dog team."

"Hi, Noah," said Keisha with a smile. "Nice to meet you."

"Hi," Noah replied.

"Sean tells me you just got home from the hospital yesterday," said Keisha.

"Yes, I hurt my leg," said Noah. "It's in a cast while my bones heal."

Just then, Link woofed. "I think Link is trying to get Angel's attention," said Noah.

Angel walked over to the sofa, and the two dogs touched noses. Then Keisha reached down to pet the French bulldog. "Link, you're always such a happy little guy," said Keisha.

Link's whole body moved as he wagged his stubby tail back and forth.

"Link seems to be happy everywhere he goes," replied Noah.

"Sean mentioned you'll be joining us at the library," said Keisha.

"Yes," replied Noah as Link rolled around on the blankets. "I can't wait to meet the other comfort dogs."

"Even better," said his grandmother. "Keisha and Angel will be staying with us tonight while the comfort team is in town."

"Wow," replied Noah, amazed to think that this beautiful dog would be their guest.

The golden retriever gently placed her head on Noah's cast and looked up at him with her warm, brown eyes. Despite her large size, Angel was very gentle. She somehow seemed to know that Noah had hurt his leg.

"Nice to meet you, Angel," said Noah. He reached out his hand and petted her head. Noah couldn't believe how soft and silky her fur was. And it was a beautiful pale yellow color—almost the same exact color as Wheaty O's, his favorite cereal.

While he was stroking her silky fur, Noah felt a nudge. It was Link pushing his nose into Noah's other hand.

"Don't worry, Link," said Noah, rubbing his belly. "You'll be getting plenty of attention, too."

In the kitchen, Noah's grandmother set the table for breakfast. When Noah limped to the table and sat down, Link settled at his feet. Next to Noah sat Keisha, with Angel plopping down nearby.

Before Nana served the breakfast, she placed a plate of dog biscuits on the floor. Link and Angel both jumped up and grabbed a biscuit. Link carried his treat to the couch, where he immediately tried to bury it in the cushions. Angel gobbled hers down right away.

Then Nana placed a platter of warm biscuits, fried eggs, and fruit on the table. Noah ate his biscuit in two quick bites. "You and Angel both love biscuits, I see," Keisha said, smiling. Everyone laughed.

"So, did Angel get special training to be a comfort dog?" Nana asked Keisha.

"Oh, yes," replied Noah. "Comfort dogs start training at eight weeks old. They learn how to follow **commands** and not be afraid of new people or places. When they learn all the special skills they need for the job, then they get a **certificate**."

"I was asking Keisha," said Nana with a laugh. "But now you sound like an **expert**!"

"I learned a lot from Sean's book," said Noah. "And Link's taught me a few things about comfort dogs, too."

19

CHAPTER 4

The Team Arrives

The library was full of people from Barkley when Noah and Nana arrived. The adults looked tired and talked among themselves. At the tables along the walls, the kids sat quietly.

Then Angel and Link entered with their handlers, and there was a buzz of excitement. As the kids were hurrying toward them, the other comfort dogs arrived. The handlers introduced their dogs one by one.

"Hi, kids," said one of the handlers. "This is Ginger and Marley. Ginger, like Angel over there, is a golden retriever, and Marley is a Labrador retriever."

Another handler introduced a dog with dark gray curls. "And this is Alma. She's what you call a standard poodle."

Then there was a huge Saint Bernard. "Hi, everybody," said his handler. "This is Winston, and I think he needs a hug."

Three of the younger kids ran to Winston with open arms. They could barely reach across his chest. While they were hugging him, Noah moved around the room in his wheelchair with Link on his lap. A lot of kids came up to Noah to pet Link and ask questions. Then Marley, the black Lab, crossed the room to where one child sat alone.

He gently placed his head on the boy's knee. The boy smiled and stroked the Lab's shiny black fur. Marley wagged his tail.

Watching them, Noah understood the special talent these comfort dogs had. Link had done a great job making him feel better. But this **canine** team knew how to help heal a *whole town*. Even the grown-ups, who had seemed so serious, were smiling. Noah looked around the room for his grandmother and wheeled over to her.

"You know, Nana, with the comfort dogs here, everybody's feeling better," said Noah. "I wish Mom could be here to see this."

"Wishes have a funny way of coming true," replied his grandmother, looking toward the entrance of the library.

Noah spotted his mom entering the building wearing an orange volunteer vest. Her black hair was stuffed under a baseball cap. Noah excitedly wheeled across the room to hug her. She reached out and kissed his forehead. Link stood up with two paws on the arm of the wheelchair.

"Mom, this is Link," said Noah.

"Hey there, Link! What a handsome dog," said Noah's mom. "And I want you to meet my new friend." His mom held up a pet carrier. Two eyes peered out at Noah, and a flat furry nose wiggled. Link stretched toward the cage, sniffing the air to identify the strange creature.

"Is that the rabbit you rescued?" asked Noah, remembering the news.

"Yes," replied his mom. "She'll be staying with us until we find her owners."

A friend of Noah's from Barkley approached them, holding a pen. "Hi, Noah. Can I sign your cast?" she asked.

"Sure," he said. First she wrote her name, *Aliyah*, then she drew a cartoon kitten with a black spot on its face.

"Aliyah, is that Meep?" asked Noah. He recognized the kitten whom he had helped Aliyah name.

"Meep is an unusual name," said Noah's mom.

"We named her Meep because when she meows that's how it sounds," Noah replied.

"Yes," said Aliyah sadly. "But she's been missing since the storm."

"I'm so sorry," said Noah's mom. "But the volunteers are still working. Maybe they will find your kitty."

"I hope so," replied Aliyah, her eyes filling with tears.

"Would you like to hold Link?" asked Noah.

"Yes," she replied, taking Link in her arms. As she held Link, he licked her nose, and a smile spread across Aliyah's face.

Just then Keisha and Angel joined them. "Nice job," Keisha whispered to Noah. "I think you'd make a great comfort dog handler."

"Me, too," replied Noah, smiling.

CHAPTER 5

Going Home

When Noah awoke on Nana's sofa the next day, he heard Angel yapping nearby. Although she was asleep on the rug, her paws were twitching.

"Is she okay?" Noah asked Keisha, who was standing in the doorway.

"Angel's fine," she said. "Did you know that dogs dream, just like people? She's probably dreaming about being back home in Oklahoma running across our yard," Keisha said, smiling.

"Is that where you're going next—back home?" asked Noah.

"Not yet," said Keisha. "Later today, we're flying out west with some of the other comfort dogs and their handlers."

"Where out west?" asked Noah.

"California," Keisha replied. "You might have seen on the news that there's a big wildfire that has destroyed many homes. We're going there to meet with the **displaced** families."

Just then, the doorbell rang, waking up Angel, who stretched and yawned. It was Sean and Link. Noah's grandmother greeted Sean and led him back to the living room.

"Good morning, everybody," said Sean. "We just stopped by to say good-bye to Keisha and Angel."

"How's Link doing today?" asked Keisha.

"See for yourself," said Sean as Link sniffed and nudged Angel to get up and play. Still tired, Angel gently pushed Link away with her paws.

"He certainly is a lively little dog," Keisha said with a laugh.

Link trotted over to Noah who picked him up. Playfully, Link wrestled and kicked out his hind legs.

"Yes, it's hard to believe he'll be eleven years old next month," said Sean.

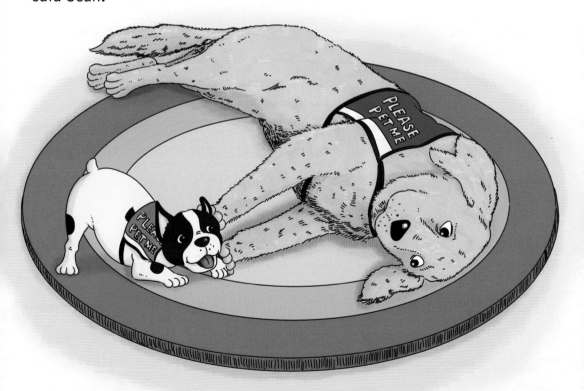

"Eleven?" asked Nana with a smile. "But Link still acts like a pup."

"Yes," agreed Sean. "But the time has come for Link to **retire**. It's getting difficult for him to travel."

"Retire?" exclaimed Noah. "But he loves his work, and he's so good at being a comfort dog."

"We'll still visit Hound Town Hospital every week," said Sean. "And of course you'll see us at the library. Link loves being with the kids during story hour. But his traveling days are over."

"Sean," said Noah, "when you and Link visit the hospital, can I go with you?"

"Of course," replied Sean. "You two make a great team. You both have huge hearts!"

That afternoon, Noah's grandmother drove Keisha and Angel to the airport. Sean and Link rode with Noah in the backseat. The other handlers were outside the airport with their dogs when Nana's jeep pulled up. As Noah approached them on his crutches, Marley the Labrador gave a sharp bark.

"Great to see you again, Marley," said Noah.

The dogs waited calmly beside their owners. Noah said his good-byes to the team and hugged Keisha and Angel.

When they got back into the jeep, Nana turned to Noah. "Let's check out your neighborhood. Your mom called and said that the roads have reopened."

For the first time in a week, patches of blue appeared in the sky. As Nana drove into Barkley, Noah and Sean could see traces of the storm. At Noah's school, workers were repairing the damaged roof. People were still clearing away **debris** in the yards of their homes.

Nana drove up to Noah's house. The water had finally **receded**, except for a small stream that ran alongside the driveway. When Noah opened the car door, Link immediately jumped out. He ran to the stream and started barking wildly.

"What's got you so excited?" asked Sean.

Noah looked toward the stream. There he saw a small animal with a hard round shell sunning itself on a rock.

"Is that the tortoise you told me about in the hospital?" asked Sean.

"Oh my gosh. That's him . . . That's Tank!" Noah replied. Link kept barking and began to run around the tortoise in circles.

After Noah got out of the jeep and bent down to pick up Tank, he heard a small high-pitched sound coming from a nearby tree.

Meeeeeep. Meeeeeep.

"Did you guys just hear that?" asked Noah. He turned around and looked up. Among the leafy branches of the willow tree, Noah spotted a tiny kitten with a patch of black fur on its face.

"I can't believe it. That's Aliyah's kitten!" shouted Noah.

"Are you sure?" asked his grandmother.

"I'm positive. I can recognize that meow anywhere," said Noah.

Sean asked Noah to borrow one of his crutches. Then Sean leaned the crutch on the tree. "Come, kitty," he called. The kitten hesitated and then slowly climbed onto the crutch's wide rubber top. Carefully, Sean lowered Meep from the branch and handed the squirming kitten to Noah. Link barked and jumped around in the grass.

"See, Noah?" Nana said. "These animals are survivors—just like you!" Then she leaned over and gave Noah a big hug. "A little bravery goes a long way."

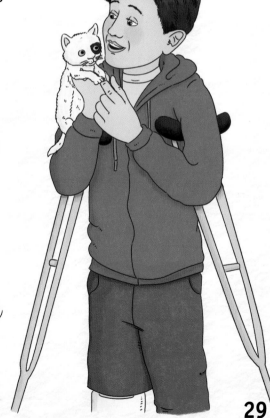

Noah and Link
A Comfort Dog Story

1. List three words that describe both Noah and Link.

2. After the flood in Barkley, how did Noah's mother and the other volunteers help out?

3. Think about the team of comfort dogs that visited Hound Town. Although the dogs were all different breeds, how were they alike?

4. If you had a comfort dog, what do you think it would be like helping people in need? Would it be stressful, rewarding, or both? Why?

GLOSSARY

burrowed (BUHR-ohd) hid beneath

canine (KAY-nine) a member of the dog family

certificate (sur-TIF-uh-kit) a piece of paper that states a program has been completed

commands (kuh-MANDZ) orders given by someone

courageous (kuh-RAY-juhss) brave

debris (duh-BREE) the broken pieces of something

displaced (diss-PLAYST) when people are forced to move out of their homes

evacuated (i-VAK-yoo-ay-ted) moved people away from an area because it's dangerous

expert (EK-spurt) someone who knows a lot about something

handler (HAND-lur) a person who helps train or manage a dog

natural disasters (NACH-ur-uhl duh-ZASS-turz) events caused by weather or nature that result in great damage or loss

nudged (nuhjd) touched or pushed away gently

receded (ri-SEED-uhd) moved back

retire (ri-TIRE) to stop working

rewarding (ree-WARD-ing) giving you a good feeling that you have done something right

stranded (STRAND-id) left in a lonely or dangerous position

traumatic (truh-MAT-ik) emotionally disturbing

tremors (TREM-urz) shaking caused by an earthquake

uniform (YU-nih-form) a special kind of clothing worn by a group or team

victims (VIK-tuhms) people or animals who are hurt or killed

volunteers (vol-uhn-TIHRZ) people who help others for free

About the Author

E. Merwin writes stories, poems, and books for kids and adults. She thanks the 9 dogs in her life (and one litter of 12 puppies born in her Brooklyn bathtub) for teaching her so much about dog behavior.

About the Illustrator

Anthony Lewis graduated from the Liverpool School of Art and Design with an honors degree in illustration. Since then, he has illustrated more than 400 children's books, ranging from simple board books to large anthologies. Anthony has traveled to many countries to research the books he illustrates. He lives in a small rural village in Cheshire, England, with his wife Kathryn, who's a graphic designer, and his children, Isabella, Emilia, and Rory, and two cats, Diesel and Harry.